For
Tubby-toes, Hawthorn and Pteddy
who all like picnics

The artist would like to thank
The Bethnal Green Museum of Childhood,
Arundel Toy and Military Museum
and the Bear Museum, Petersfield
for the inspiration for many of the
bears portrayed in this book.

Published by
Peter Bedrick Books
2112 Broadway
New York, NY 10023

Published by agreement with Penguin Books, UK
Printed in the United States of America.

10 9 8 7 95 96 97 98 99 00

Library of Congress Cataloguing-in-Publication Data
Kennedy, Jimmy
    The teddy bears' picnic.
    Summary: presents the texts of the familiar song
about the festivities at the teddy-bears'-picnic
    1. Children's song   2. Text.   1. Teddy bears—poetry.
    2. Picknicking—poetry.   3. Songs
    I. Theobalds.   Prue, ill.   II. Title
    PZ8.3.K383Te 1987   [E]   86-32111

ISBN 0-87226-424-6 (Pbk)

The Teddy Bears' Picnic

Pictures by
Prue Theobalds

Words by
Jimmy Kennedy

PETER BEDRICK BOOKS

NEW YORK

If you go down in the woods today
You're sure of a big surprise.

If you go down in the woods today
You'd better go in disguise;

For ev'ry Bear that ever there was
Will gather there for certain, because
Today's the day the Teddy Bears have their picnic.

Ev'ry Teddy Bear who's been good
Is sure of a treat today.

There's lots of marvellous things to eat,

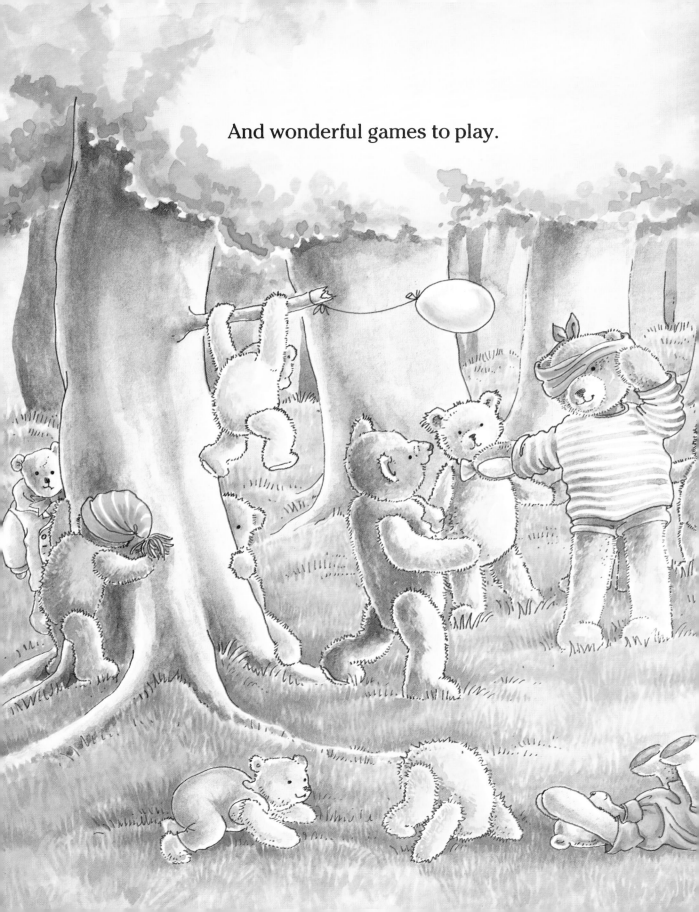

And wonderful games to play.

Beneath the trees where nobody sees
They'll hide and seek as long as they please,
'Cause that's the way the Teddy Bears have their picnic.

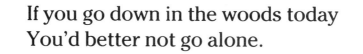

If you go down in the woods today
You'd better not go alone.

It's lovely down in the woods today
But safer to stay at home.

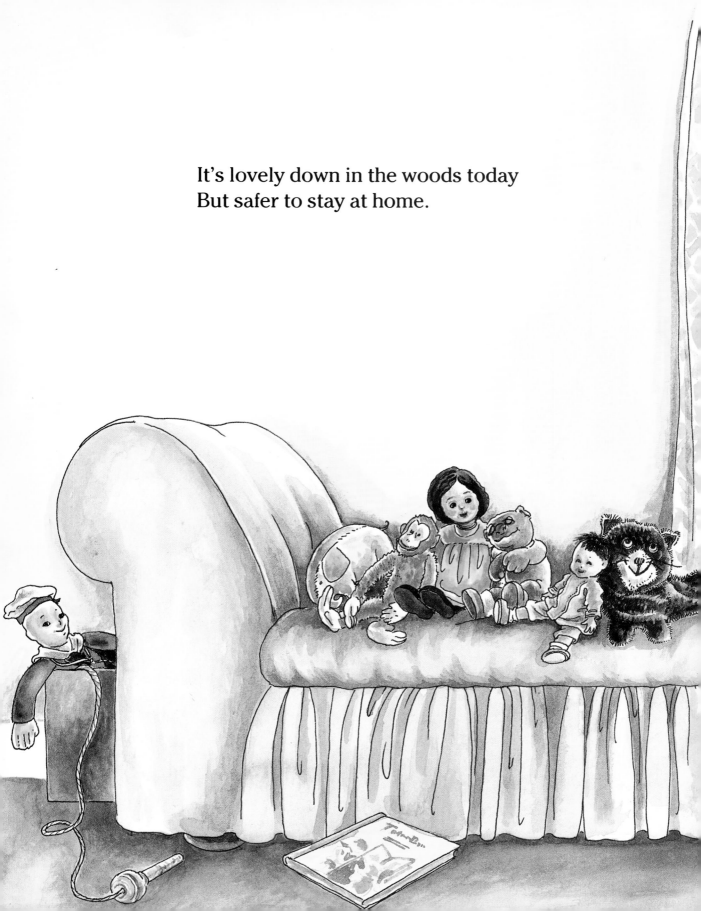

For ev'ry Bear that ever there was

Will gather there for certain, because
Today's the day the Teddy Bears have their picnic.

Picnic time for Teddy Bears,

The little Teddy Bears are having a lovely time today.
Watch them, catch them unawares
And see them picnic on their holiday.

See them gaily gad about,
They love to play and shout;
They never have any care;

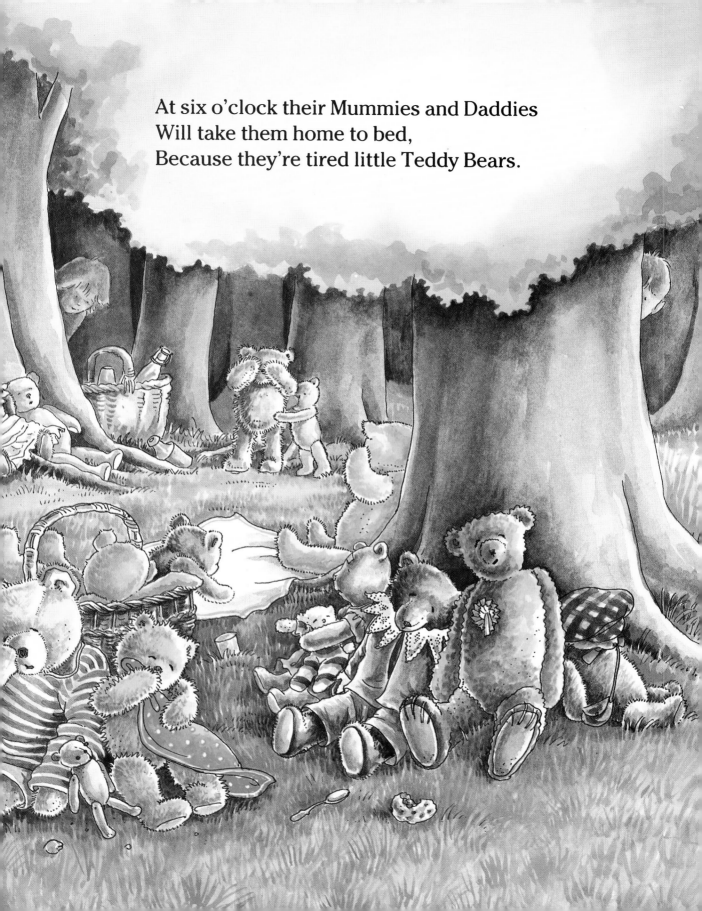

At six o'clock their Mummies and Daddies
Will take them home to bed,
Because they're tired little Teddy Bears.